OCT   2023

I AM A DRAGON!

A Squabble & a Quibble

by Sabina Hahn

HARPER
An Imprint of HarperCollinsPublishers

DRAGONS DON'T EXIST.

YOU ARE A FROG.

EVERYBODY KNOWS THAT DRAGONS, UNICORNS, GIRAFFES, AND CUPCAKES ARE IMAGINARY.

MY MOM TOLD ME.

YOUR MOM KNOWS EVERYTHING!

I MEAN, THEY ARE EITHER CUPS OR CAKES, NOT BOTH!

EXACTLY.

IT IS SO SAD! YOU DON'T KNOW WHO YOU ARE.
SO SAD.
SO WE WILL TELL YOU.
— YOU ARE A FROG.

A. DRAGON.
A VERY MAD DRAGON!

Dedicated to all the frogs
and all the dragons everywhere.

I Am a Dragon!

Copyright © 2023 by Sabina Hahn

All rights reserved. Manufactured in Italy.

No part of this book may be used or reproduced in any manner whatsoever without written permission except in the
case of brief quotations embodied in critical articles and reviews. For information address HarperCollins Children's
Books, a division of HarperCollins Publishers, 195 Broadway, New York, NY 10007.

www.harpercollinschildrens.com

Library of Congress Control Number: 2022947989

ISBN 978-0-06-325399-5

The artist used ink and watercolors to create the illustrations for this book.

Hand lettering by Sabina Hahn

Book design by Dana Fritts

23 24 25 26 27 RTLO 10 9 8 7 6 5 4 3 2 1

First Edition